JOHN J. BACH BRANCH
ALBANY PUBLIC LIBRARY

 W9-COG-270

DRAGONS

DRAGONATOMY

by *Matt Doeden*
illustrated by Jonathan Mayer

Consultant
Dr. Peter Hogarth
Professor, Department of Biology
University of York, United Kingdom

Capstone
press

Mankato, Minnesota

Edge Books are published by Capstone Press,
151 Good Counsel Drive, P.O. Box 669, Mankato, Minnesota 56002.
www.capstonepress.com

Copyright © 2008 by Capstone Press, a Capstone Publishers company.
All rights reserved. No part of this publication may be reproduced in whole
or in part, or stored in a retrieval system, or transmitted in any form or by
any means, electronic, mechanical, photocopying, recording, or otherwise,
without written permission of the publisher.
For information regarding permission, write to Capstone Press,
151 Good Counsel Drive, P.O. Box 669, Dept. R, Mankato, Minnesota 56002.
Printed in the United States of America

Library of Congress Cataloging-in-Publication Data
Doeden, Matt.
    Dragonatomy / by Matt Doeden; illustrated by Jonathan Mayer.
    p. cm. — (Edge books. Dragons)
    Summary: "Describes the different parts of dragon bodies and how dragons
breathe fire" — Provided by publisher.
    Includes bibliographical references and index.
    ISBN–13: 978-1-4296-1295-1 (hardcover)
    ISBN–10: 1-4296-1295-9 (hardcover)
    1. Dragons — Juvenile literature. I. Mayer, Jonathan, 1984– ill. II. Title. III. Series.
GR830.D7D64 2008
398.24'54 — dc22   2007025094

Editorial Credits
Aaron Sautter, editor; Ted Williams, designer; Tod Smith, diagram illustrator;
    Krista Ward, colorist

Photo Credits
Shutterstock/abzora, backgrounds; Andrey Zyk, backgrounds

1 2 3 4 5 6 13 12 11 10 09 08

TABLE OF CONTENTS

CHAPTER ONE

A Deadly Encounter

An armored knight stands on a wind-swept plain. His eyes watch the sky as a dark shadow approaches. Above him, a huge dragon stretches out its wings. The dragon shrieks as it dives at its enemy.

The dragon opens its jaws to unleash a stream of flame. The knight quickly ducks behind his dragon-scale shield. He knows how tough dragon scales are. They can protect him from the dragon's deadly fire.

The dragon turns to make another pass. It sees the long, sharp lance the knight holds. But even from a distance, the dragon can smell the human's fear.

Once more, it dives at the knight. The brave warrior braces himself, ready to thrust the steel-tipped lance into the dragon's belly. He knows the beast's weakest spot is found there. But the dragon's speed surprises the knight. The monster is upon him before he can strike. The dragon slashes with its vicious claws. It tears through the knight's armor and into his flesh. The knight falls to the ground, gasping in pain.

Again, the dragon circles. Finally, it decides the human has learned his lesson. The battle has made the dragon hungry. Deadly **venom** drips from its teeth as it flies off in search of a tasty cow.

Survival of the Fittest

It's fun to think of dragons as real creatures, rather than imaginary beasts. They are fierce, deadly foes for even the bravest dragon slayers. With fiery breath, razor-sharp teeth, and high intelligence, they are almost impossible to kill. From head to tail, dragons are built for survival.

> **venom** – a poisonous liquid that is injected into prey

CHAPTER TWO

A Head For Fighting

Powerful wings, armorlike scales, and savage claws all make dragons fearsome creatures. But with deadly breath and razor-sharp teeth, a dragon's mouth is its most dangerous feature.

Breathing Fire

Dragons are famous for their flaming breath. But not all dragons breathe fire. Frost dragons blast icy air from their mouths, while other dragons spit acid or venom. Some dragons have no breath weapon at all.

DRAGON FACT

Some dragons use their fiery breath to cook their food before they eat it.

Fire glands

Nobody knows how dragons breathe fire. One idea is that they can produce and store large amounts of hydrogen gas. Hydrogen burns easily. When they feel threatened, dragons blow out the hydrogen to create a fiery blast. How they light the gas is a mystery.

Another idea is that dragons have special glands in their mouths. The glands create and store flammable chemicals. The dragons spray the chemicals into the air, where they mix and burst into flame. Dragons don't get burned when they breathe fire. Thick layers of mucus in their mouths protect them from the intense heat.

Icy Breath

Frost dragons have a breath weapon similar to their fire-breathing cousins. Some frost dragons spray chemicals that create an icy-cold effect when mixed together. The chemical mixture quickly absorbs heat to freeze anything it touches.

A few frost dragons use another way to create freezing breath. They blow out gas that is under high pressure. As pressurized gas expands, it cools very quickly. The result is an icy blast that quickly freezes everything in its path.

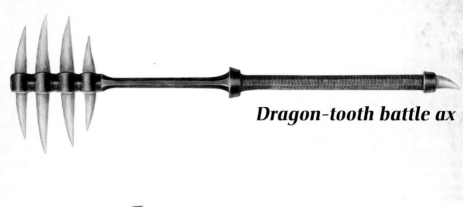

Dragon-tooth battle ax

Dragon-tooth dagger

Jaws of Steel

Dragons' jaws are just as deadly as their fiery breath. Strong jaw muscles make their mouths like steel traps. Dragons are predators. Their jaws are built for snapping bones and crushing prey.

Dragon teeth are long, sharp, and often jagged. A dragon's teeth can easily tear through a warrior's armor. The largest dragon teeth are nearly 1 foot (0.3 meters) long. Legends say that skilled weapon smiths once created rare and deadly weapons out of dragon teeth.

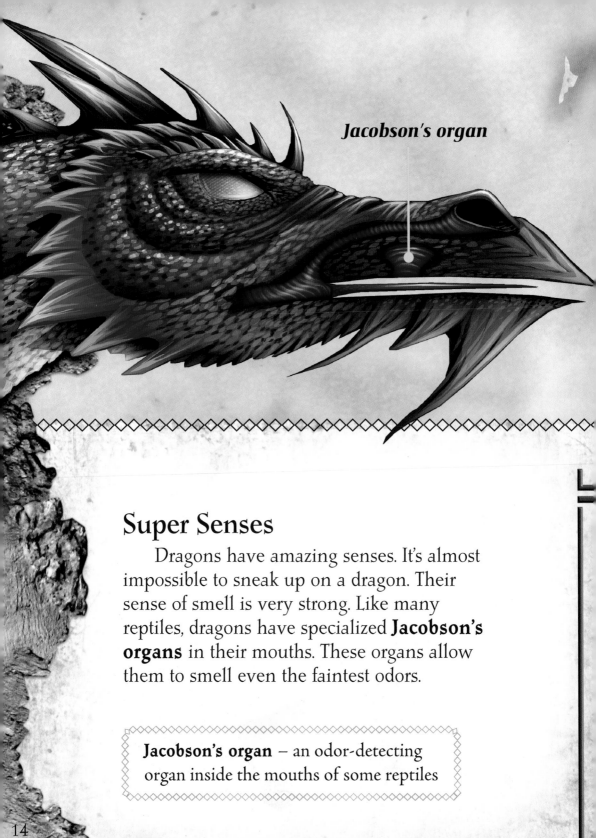

Jacobson's organ

Super Senses

Dragons have amazing senses. It's almost impossible to sneak up on a dragon. Their sense of smell is very strong. Like many reptiles, dragons have specialized **Jacobson's organs** in their mouths. These organs allow them to smell even the faintest odors.

Jacobson's organ – an odor-detecting organ inside the mouths of some reptiles

Dragons also hear well. But their small ears are only part of their sense of hearing. Their huge bodies can feel small vibrations in the ground. This ability lets dragons know when something is moving around in their **lair**. Human footsteps, for example, will quickly gain their attention.

lair – a place where a wild animal lives and sleeps

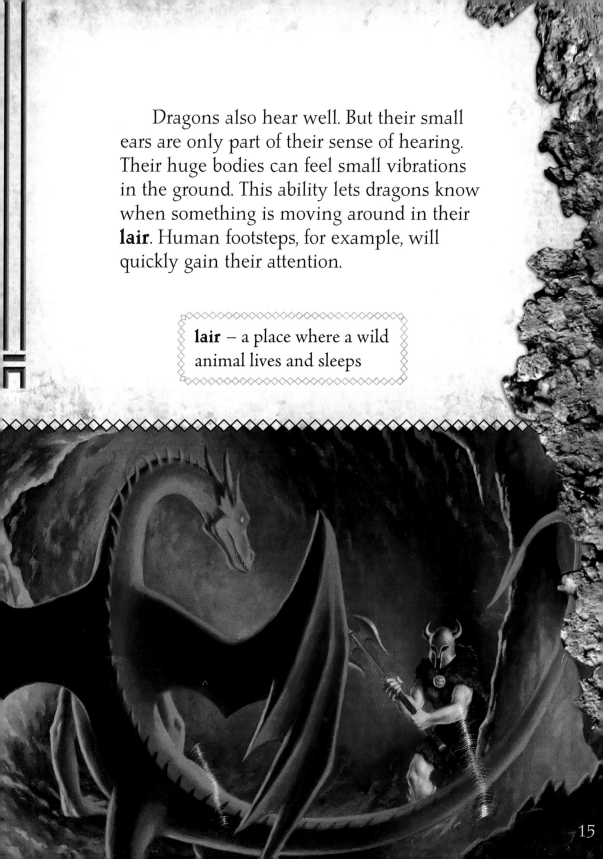

Dragons have sharp vision. Their large eyes can see motion and color from great distances. They also have excellent night vision, which is why most dragons hunt after dark. And unlike people, dragons can see both infrared and ultraviolet light. This may help explain why some dragons seem to have magical powers.

Not much is known about dragons' other senses. Their heavy, thick scales probably dull their sense of touch. They probably don't have a strong sense of taste, since they swallow most food whole. Some people believe dragons can tap into forces unknown to humans. When they do, they seem able to create and do things magically.

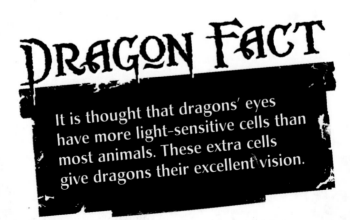

DRAGON FACT

It is thought that dragons' eyes have more light-sensitive cells than most animals. These extra cells give dragons their excellent vision.

17

CHAPTER THREE

Winged Wonders

If dragons were real, few sights would be as amazing as seeing one soaring on its outstretched wings. Most dragons' wings are tough and leathery. A few have wings covered in feathers. But they are all excellent fliers.

A Light Frame

One of the keys to understanding how dragons fly is found in their skeletons. Dragon bones are similar to a bird's. They are partially hollow and very strong. These lightweight bones help create a strong frame to support a dragon's body in flight.

Most flying dragons have muscular, streamlined bodies. Their long necks and lean frames make them **aerodynamic**. Like falcons, dragons reach great speeds while in controlled dives. This helps them catch their prey by surprise.

aerodynamic – designed to move easily through the air

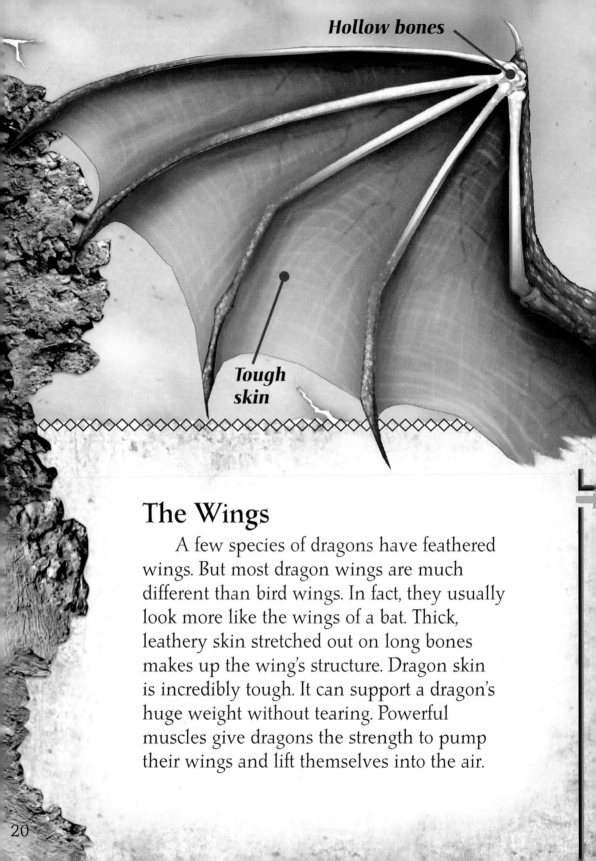

Hollow bones

Tough skin

The Wings

A few species of dragons have feathered wings. But most dragon wings are much different than bird wings. In fact, they usually look more like the wings of a bat. Thick, leathery skin stretched out on long bones makes up the wing's structure. Dragon skin is incredibly tough. It can support a dragon's huge weight without tearing. Powerful muscles give dragons the strength to pump their wings and lift themselves into the air.

In spite of their huge wings and light frame, some people think dragons shouldn't be able to fly. They are simply too large. Still, they fly anyway. How is this possible? Some think it's related to a dragon's ability to breathe fire. If dragons store hydrogen gas, some of it might be found inside their hollow bones. Hydrogen is lighter than air. It probably helps reduce a dragon's weight, making it easier to fly.

Not all dragons are created equally. Many fly with power and grace, while others can't fly at all. Many dragons don't even have wings. A few dragons have only tiny **vestigial** wings. Over the years, their wings have shrunk to the point of being useless.

Most flying creatures need wings to fly. But it seems that a few dragons can fly without them. Legends in parts of Asia say that wingless, serpentlike dragons often take to the air. Some people think these dragons must use magic to soar through the sky.

vestigial – small and undeveloped body parts

DRAGON FACT

The feet of some water dragons have turned into fins over the years.

24

CHAPTER FOUR

BUILT FOR BATTLE

Dragons have incredibly strong bodies. Their tough scales and natural weapons help dragons live for hundreds of years. These beasts also don't seem to be affected by disease or old age. No one knows of a single dragon dying of natural causes.

Tough Scales

A few dragons wear steel armor. But most dragons' scales provide plenty of protection from a sharp sword or a lance. Most dragon scales are made of a hard substance called **keratin**. This is the same material that makes up a person's fingernails. But a dragon's scales are much thicker and denser. In rare cases, the keratin is combined with metal to make the scales even stronger.

> **keratin** – a hard substance that forms certain body parts

Overlapping scales

Unlike most reptiles, dragons do not shed their skin as they grow. New scales constantly grow under the old ones. When old scales fall off, new ones are ready to take their place. This is an important difference. If dragons did shed their skin, they'd be left with little protection for several days.

DRAGON FACT

Dragon slayers prize dragon scales. Since scales resist both dragon fire and dragon magic, they make great shields.

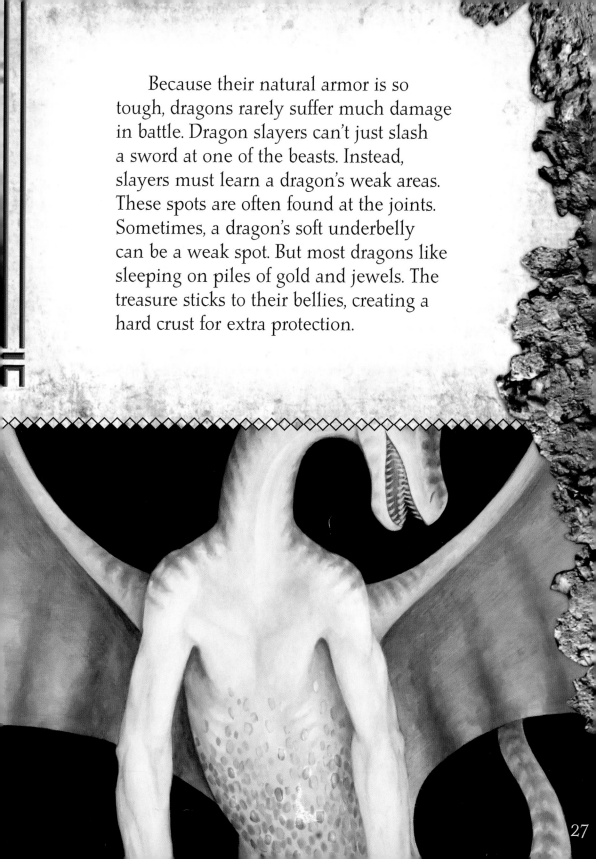

Because their natural armor is so tough, dragons rarely suffer much damage in battle. Dragon slayers can't just slash a sword at one of the beasts. Instead, slayers must learn a dragon's weak areas. These spots are often found at the joints. Sometimes, a dragon's soft underbelly can be a weak spot. But most dragons like sleeping on piles of gold and jewels. The treasure sticks to their bellies, creating a hard crust for extra protection.

Claws and Tail

Blazing fire and huge teeth aren't a dragon's only weapons. Whether dragons have two legs or four, their feet are tipped with long, pointed claws. These savage claws can rip both prey and enemies to shreds. Four-legged dragons also have thumbs on their front feet. This allows them to grip and use items just like people can. Although these dragons don't need to carry extra weapons, they could if they wanted to.

Dragon tails are incredibly powerful. They are also very flexible. Dragon tails are good for gripping and fighting. Dragons often use their strong, whiplike tails for deadly surprise attacks. Many dragon slayers have been bashed by a wicked tail slap during a fierce battle.

Everything about a dragon's body is impressive. From head to tail, dragons are built to survive. They are fast, strong, and smart. It's no wonder dragon legends have spread around the world. No beast, real or imagined, is as powerful or majestic as the dragon.

GLOSSARY

aerodynamic (air-oh-dye-NA-mik) — designed to move easily through the air

flammable (FLAM-uh-buhl) — likely to catch fire

Jacobson's organ (JAY-kuhb-sunz OR-gun) — an odor-detecting organ inside the mouths of some reptiles

keratin (KAIR-uh-tin) — the hard substance that forms hair and fingernails; dragon scales are also made of keratin.

lair (LAIR) — a place where a wild animal lives and sleeps

mucus (MYOO-kuhss) — sticky, wet liquid made by glands to protect parts of the body

venom (VEN-uhm) — a poisonous liquid produced by some animals that is injected into prey

vestigial (VEST-uh-gil) — small and undeveloped; vestigial body parts are not useful.

Read More

Steer, Dugald, ed. *Dr. Ernest Drake's Dragonology: The Complete Book of Dragons.* Cambridge, Mass.: Candlewick Press, 2003.

Topsell, John. *How to Raise and Keep a Dragon.* Hauppauge, N. Y.: Barrons Educational Series, 2006.

Trumbauer, Lisa. *A Practical Guide to Dragons.* Renton, Wash.: Wizards of the Coast, 2006.

Internet Sites

FactHound offers a safe, fun way to find Internet sites related to this book. All of the sites on FactHound have been researched by our staff.

Here's how:
1. Visit *www.facthound.com*
2. Choose your grade level.
3. Type in this book ID **1429612959** for age-appropriate sites. You may also browse subjects by clicking on letters, or by clicking on pictures and words.
4. Click on the **Fetch It** button.

FactHound will fetch the best sites for you!

INDEX